Dear Parent:

Your child's love of reading starts here!

Every child learns to read in a different way and at his or her own speed. Some go back and forth between reading levels and read favorite books again and again. Others read through each level in order. You can help your young reader improve and become more confident by encouraging his or her own interests and abilities. From books your child reads with you to the first books he or she reads alone, there are I Can Read Books for every stage of reading:

SHARED READING
Basic language, word repetition, and whimsical illustrations, ideal for sharing with your emergent reader

BEGINNING READING
Short sentences, familiar words, and simple concepts for children eager to read on their own

READING WITH HELP
Engaging stories, longer sentences, and language play for developing readers

READING ALONE
Complex plots, challenging vocabulary, and high-interest topics for the independent reader

I Can Read Books have introduced children to the joy of reading since 1957. Featuring award-winning authors and illustrators and a fabulous cast of beloved characters, I Can Read Books set the standard for beginning readers.

A lifetime of discovery begins with the magical words "I Can Read!"

Visit www.icanread.com for information
on enriching your child's reading experience.

To Ruthie,
forever a lover of travel
and making new friends
—T.B.

I Can Read Book® is a trademark of HarperCollins Publishers.

Little Penguin's New Friend
Copyright © 2019 by Tadgh Bentley
All rights reserved. Manufactured in the United States of America.
No part of this book may be used or reproduced in any manner whatsoever without written permission except
in the case of brief quotations embodied in critical articles and reviews. For information address HarperCollins
Children's Books, a division of HarperCollins Publishers, 195 Broadway, New York, NY 10007.
www.icanread.com

Library of Congress Control Number: 2018958891
ISBN 978-0-06-269995-4 (trade bdg.) —ISBN 978-0-06-269994-7 (pbk.)

Book design by Dana Fritts and Andrea Vandergrift
19 20 21 22 23 LSCC 10 9 8 7 6 5 4 3 2   ❖   First Edition

I Can Read!

Little Penguin's New Friend

Story by Laura Driscoll
Pictures by Tadgh Bentley

HARPER

An Imprint of HarperCollinsPublishers

Oh! Hi! Sorry!

I did not see you there.

You see, we are all talking

about the big news.

A polar bear is coming to visit!

I know what you are thinking.

Polar bears live at the North Pole.

Penguins live at the South Pole.

So we have never met a polar bear.

I wonder what they are like.

Kenneth says

polar bears have sharp teeth

and terrifying roars.

Claude has heard

polar bears are mean hunters!

And Franklin has heard
polar bears tell bad jokes.
Very bad jokes.

But I am not worried.

Do you know why?

I once heard this advice.

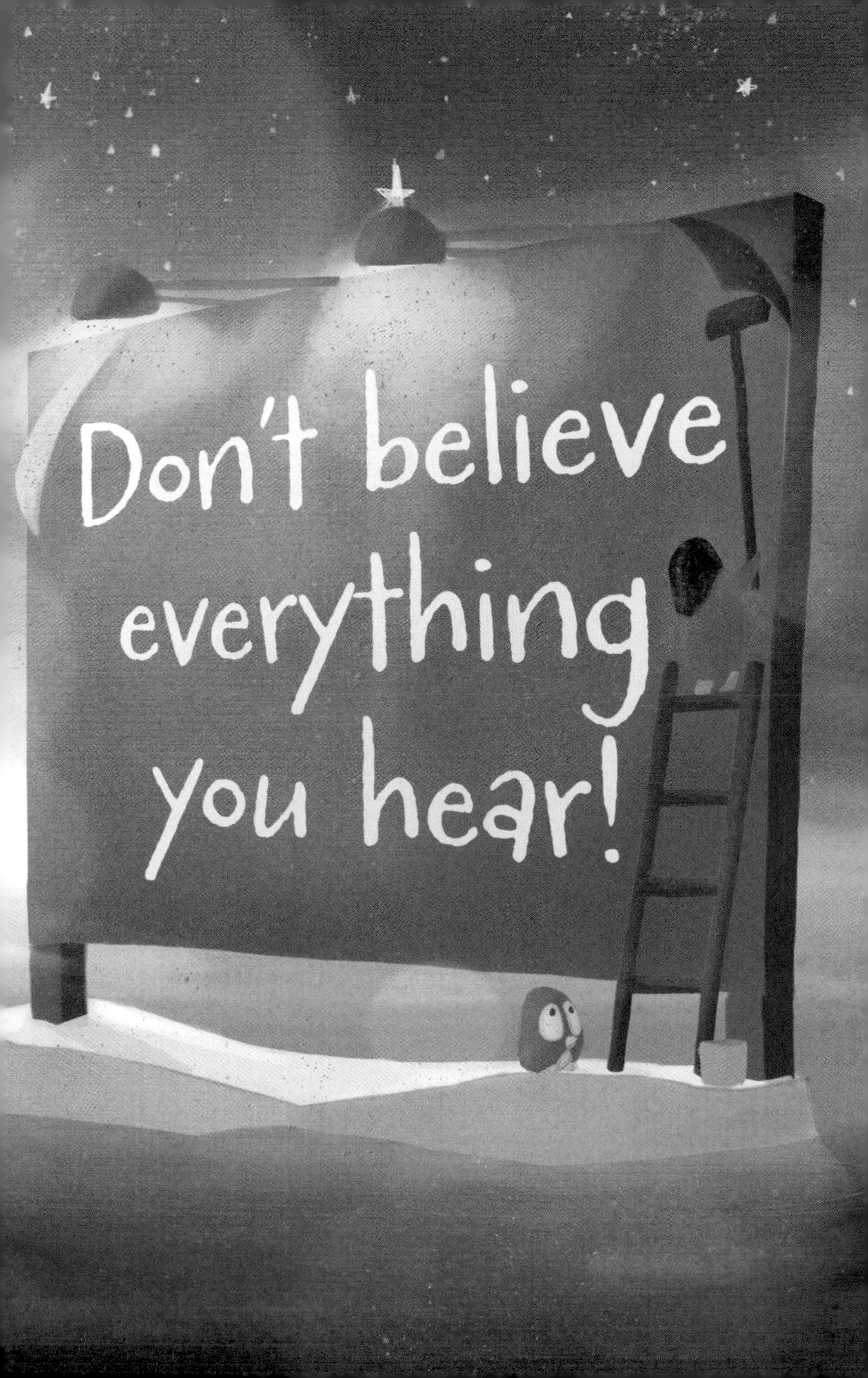
Don't believe
everything
you hear!

After all,

they call Franklin

a *killer* whale.

But we are best friends.

Look!

Here comes a ship now!

This polar bear does
not look scary.
Her teeth are sharp.
But they are no sharper
than Franklin's.

The polar bear *is* roaring—

with laughter!

That is not scary at all.

She looks perfectly nice.

"Welcome, Polar Bear," I say.

"I am Little Penguin."

"Hello, Little Penguin,"
Polar Bear says.
"A question for you!
What time should I go
to the dentist?"

"The dentist?" I say.

I am confused.

But Polar Bear answers for me.

"Tooth hurty!" she says.

She roars with laughter again.

"Get it?

Tooth hurty?

Like two thirty?"

AAAAAAAAAAH!

Do you know what that was?

That was a bad joke.

A very, very bad joke!

Polar bears *do* tell bad jokes!

It is true!

And if *that* is true…

are polar bears mean hunters,

after all?

Polar Bear
by Claude

EEK!

The polar bear is after me!

I cannot look.

Does she seem hungry to you?

"It is okay!" the polar bear says.

"I have other jokes!

How do you keep a fish from

smelling?"

Ack!

This one is pretty bad, too.

"Plug its nose!" I shout,

as I run and dive for cover.

"Aw," Polar Bear says.

"Then I bet you know this one.

What did the zero say to the eight?"

My mind is a blank.

I do not know this one.

Do you?

"NICE BELT!" the polar bear says.

That *is* kind of funny.

"I like that one," I say.

"Phew!" the polar bear says.

"I was starting to worry."

"Why?" I ask.

The polar bear smiles.

"I heard that penguins

have no sense of humor," she says.